MW01688613

Santa Monica Christmas

THE
FARNUNG
CLAN
GOD BLESS YOUR
FOREVER FAMILY!
BOB LONSBERRY

Other Books by Bob Lonsberry

The Early Years: A Collection of Columns

Baghdad Christmas

Hopiland Christmas

A Various Language

Cumorah Christmas

Joseph Avenue Christmas

Santa Monica Christmas

a memior

By Bob Lonsberry

CANISTEO
FREE PRESS
MOUNT MORRIS, NY

ISBN: 978-1-61364-770-7

Published by:
Canisteo Free Press
Mount Morris, New York

Printed in Rochester, New York
United States of America

Cover design by Amanda Lonsberry

Dedicated to my siblings,
Sean, Peter and Natilee Liddy.

Firm in the faith that they will again and eternally be
in the loving arms of their dear mother and father.

Chapter One

She got out of the state hospital a year before they went to California.

I joined them two years after that, just after I turned 6, the summer that Watts burned. At night, he stood on the porch with the neighbor men and watched the flame on the horizon with a pistol in his hand. By day the great plume of ruin and hate moved east with the inland breeze. By night he and the neighbor men milled around to make sure that what was happening over there stayed over there.

He was heavyset and 34. This was his second marriage. He'd come out of a little hollow where New York bleeds into Pennsylvania and had turned 21 in Korea with the Air Force. He would be dead at the breakfast table one Saturday morning before he turned 40.

They had met at Jumbo's, above North Hornell. She was the waitress and he was the cook and for all they could see they weren't ever going to get anywhere in that little town, so they took her tips and his car and caught 66 in Chicago like all the other Okies. "Sugar Shack," "Surfin' USA," and "The End of the World" on a tinny radio in a big old boat of a finned car lumbering down the Main Streets of Missouri and Oklahoma and New Mexico and Arizona. The heat of Needles, the brown of Barstow, the ocean of Santa Monica.

That's where they settled. As close to that old pier as they could get. Santa Monica, California. Named for the mother of a prodigal who became a philosopher saint. The end of 66 and the beginning of a new life. A blue-water paradise for wide-eyed country kids, amazed at their good fortune and the oranges on the trees.

She was 24 and this was her third marriage. The first husband took off when she got pregnant for me. The second marriage, the temporary one to the village idiot, she endured to get me back.

Her mother told her when I was born that she couldn't have a baby if she didn't have a husband, and that was that. She was 18 then and I went to sleep in a drawer pulled from her mother's dresser, and she went to live at the state hospital.

It was probably her second breakdown.

That's what they were called back then. Nervous breakdowns. A simple phrase to describe a horrifying malfunction of the mind. She had had her first right after her mother had had hers, when the seven kids were farmed out and she, a little girl, was bunked in with the retarded adult son of the family that took her in.

That was the first breakdown, the first of many in a long string of episodic collapses of self, clustered sometimes, explainable sometimes, completely out of the blue sometimes, the landmarks of a life defined by mental decay and uncertainty.

But the second time is when they took me and she was driven up to the state hospital and stripped of her clothes for the louse inspection. She had to be showered and shampooed by the orderlies and they combed through and they gave her a gown and a pair of flip flops and put her out into a high-fenced yard with the others. She didn't speak a word for two years. Before she died, having smoked herself into an early emphysema, she said that it was because of the shock of not having any undergarments that first day. They turned her out in the yard in a gown with no brassiere or underwear and it made everything worse and it made everything unbearable and a decent girl shouldn't have to do that and for two years she lived in a silent, oblivious funk.

In those days, they did crafts. Shock and, for some, lobotomy, but for everyone crafts. She escaped the lobotomy but not the shock and years later when they put her on a nasal cannula she was thrilled, because she knew that patients on oxygen therapy couldn't be given shock and she was, at long last, freed from that old foe and that old fear. The crafts were mostly copper work. They were given a rectangle of malleable copper and a three-dimensional template and, securing the two together, with a dull wooden tool the copper was rubbed until it had taken on the contours of the template. The copper was then caustically aged and tacked to a piece of plywood and hung on the wall.

She gave these as gifts to relatives, in something of the manner first-graders give school art projects as gifts. A copper Last Supper hung in the living room of her mother's house, next to a kitten embossed on the same material by the same hand.

But that was some 3,000 miles away.

And 3,000 miles is a long way when you are running, when you are starting over, when you are going to a place of new beginnings and fresh starts. When each introduction is a do over, a chance to be someone you've not been before, a chance to be someone you've not been allowed to be before, 3,000 miles is the perfect distance.

They were two more from Back East. It seemed most everybody in Santa Monica was from Back East then. Back East or Down South or Mexico. At 611 Ocean Park Boulevard, an old house with one garage and three front doors, there were two families from Down South and one from Back East. The southerners were from Arkansas and Georgia, and we easterners were from New York. The people around the corner, in the first house on Beverly, were Mexican and they had the whole house to themselves. There was a girl named Chocolata who lived there, and she and I often ran together down Beverly to Joslyn Park, under the big eucalyptus trees, to swing high in the air and look over the houses and the trees at the ocean beyond.

It was the Golden State then, the land of opportunity, where streets were paved with gold, and people lived the odd paradox of painfully missing the very places they had done everything to escape. This place was their only hope, and it held their futures, but the old place was their only memory, and it held their hearts. That was evident in their speech, as most groups of chatting adults ultimately devolved into retelling stories about Back East or Down South or home in Mexico. They were pioneers, in their way, as much immigrants to this new land as if they had sailed into New York harbor or in through the Golden Gate. Except for some of them from Mexico, they all came from places where it rained and was humid and the top soil was deep and rich, and where their families had lived for generations on end. But their lot was now in the wind, the westward wind, and they had fallen to root here, in the big smoggy city with its anonymous millions and its promise of a brighter day.

Chapter Two

They started working at Clovis's across from the Boeing plant when they first came to California.

His discharge papers didn't make up for the lack of a high school diploma, and she had dropped out in the 10th grade, so when they were turned away from the hiring office at the factory, they walked across the street to the diner, and shortly thereafter he was the cook and she was the waitress.

A year later the baby came and a year later I came and that summer before I started the first-grade, while they were working, the baby and I spent our days in the backroom of Clovis's, with a pool table and the extra chairs, kegs of beer and shelves of canned goods. They named him Sean, after John Wayne in "The Quiet Man," and I learned to diaper him and give him his bottle and calm his cries as they worked from 4 in the morning till 7 at night. She took her breaks with us and peeked in when she could. He got no breaks, but carried us in his big arms at the beginning and end of the day, when we were usually asleep. She had worked through the pregnancy, and come back a week later, but it was months of tips and weekend shifts to pay off the hospital, and only when that was done could they afford a bigger place, and they moved to Ocean Park Boulevard.

Once they were there, there was room for me, and I was sent for, and I met my baby brother.

Our share of the house was three rooms, a toilet and two stoops.

On the front of the house, with its long side facing Ocean Park Boulevard to our south, was our living room. It had a fold-out couch upon which they slept, a coffee table, a black-and-white television set and a goldfish bowl. Perpendicular to that room, with its long side facing the house's west wall, was the dining room, which held the table where we ate and she mended our clothes. On the eastern wall of that room, in a recess under the stairs of the neighbor's apartment, was a wide closet from which the doors had been removed. Bunk beds had been set up half in the closet and half out. I slept on top, and Sean slept on the bottom, in a large citrus crate that served as his crib. The kitchen was attached to the dining room and the tub and toilet were on the mostly enclosed back stoop, next to their proudest possession, an old wringer washer he had bought her for $15 as a birthday present.

We went barefoot then. Most kids did. At least the ones I grew up around. In the summer, and on the weekends, if it wasn't rainy, we went barefoot. But you have to wear shoes to school, and when I was enrolled down the hill at John Muir School, I had to put back on the hard leather kindergarten shoes of the year before. I had outgrown them and they pinched and blistered and at recess I mostly stood along the fence to keep from running around and wearing sores on my feet.

John Muir was a wonderful school on the big corner where Ocean Park met the Pacific Coast Highway - or Lincoln Boulevard as it's known in that stretch. The playground was a vast expanse of pavement interspersed with tetherball poles. There was no grass, but there was an internal courtyard which several of the classrooms opened onto and where tropical trees and flowers grew and which seemed like a paradise to me.

In kindergarten, Back East, a bus had picked me up from my grandmother's house on Willow Bend Road, a big yellow bus, driven by Paul Stewart, a dairy farmer from another couple of miles outside town. His daughter Patty was in my class and she sat beside me on the bus each day. After school, my grandmother would be waiting at the house, having taken a late lunch, and would drive me back to Hornell, to the gas station and the car wash and the coin laundry, businesses in which she was a partner, clustered on a corner by a bridge over the river. It was Roy, the other partner, and Denny, the hired man, and my grandmother and me, and Roy and Denny would pump gas and check oil while I climbed on stacks of tires and an old fire engine out back and my grandmother ran the cash register.

We closed at 7 and after my grandmother counted the till at the gas station we emptied the coins from each of the washers and dryers in the laundry and, until I learned to count and roll the dimes and quarters myself, my job was to scan their edges for the pure silver ones from before 1963. After 1963, the coins had copper or something in them and there was a reddish line around the edge. The coins that lacked that line were good; they were pure silver, and we didn't roll those for the deposit, we took them home to store in coffee cans and mayonnaise jars in my grandmother's closet.

At night, my grandmother read me "Toby Tyler." But that was kindergarten Back East, and this was first-grade in California. And there was no Paul Stewart and there was no big yellow bus and John Muir School was not quite a quarter mile down the hill from our house. You crossed Beverly and you crossed Seventh and you were there, and after being shown once I was fine to go back and forth. I had a key to our place and after school I either went inside to watch "Dark Shadows" or sat on the front stoop on an old couch and read the jokes in "Boys Life." Schwinn had a new bicycle out - the Orange Krate - and it debuted in a full-page ad on the back cover of "Boys Life." I sat there afternoon after afternoon, looking at that ad, dreaming about that bike.

They called my mother out of work once, to come in and talk about a concern. As a new student, they had asked me questions. About counting and the alphabet and colors and shapes and how I looked at life. They asked me if I liked to pretend, and I said I didn't. They asked me if I ever pretended, and I said I didn't. And that was enough to call her in and she had to miss the lunch rush at Clovis's and so she was a little perturbed when that night she pulled open the middle built-in drawer in the dining room, the one full of my toys and trinkets, and asked me what I was doing in the evenings when I stood in front of that drawer and fiddled with its contents.

That's where I played. In that drawer. And that's where I kept my copy of "Boys Life" and the hardbound "Toby Tyler" my grandmother had sent with me from Back East. It was at that drawer that I stood as, late in the fall, the two of them raised their voices in exasperation over this uncle or that and the disposition of my great-grandfather's estate. He had been the worshipful master of his Masonic lodge and the superintendent of the county farm and the highway foreman when they still worked with horses and, we would learn many years later, the head of the local Ku Klux Klan. I knew him as an old man nearing 90, bent and addled, who showed me how to pick raspberries and gave me once a packet of marigold seeds that had come free with his Shredded Wheat.

He had died and left some small amount and a fight was on over who got what. This uncle wanted that and that uncle wanted this and each thought the other was a crook and a scoundrel, and that attitude played out over a couple of dozen descendants into a bitter chaos that lasted after all the adults involved were dead. Those six-thousand dollars were the worst thing he could have left, as they cankered the heart of his family and left it something less than a family.

But right then it wasn't about family or legacy, it was about light bills and car payments and what the heck are we going to feed the kids. As the two of them ranted angrily about what they could do with their share, with the three- or four-hundred dollars that might come their way, I stared into the drawer and listened, frightened by what life would later tell me was the sound of terrorized desperation.

Which is how it is when you're short. When you're always short. When payday isn't a respite, or when there isn't a payday. When you can't catch a break, when you can't catch your breath, when there is no light at the end of the tunnel. When you work to exhaustion and beyond and the hole just keeps getting deeper. Interest compounds against you, bill collectors haunt your phone and your door and your mind, and the fear that it could get even worse leaves you clinging anxiously to not much of a life at all. It all blows away in the westward wind and leaves you with nothing but the haunting gnaw of unmeetable obligation. To shelter yourself, to feed your children, to put one foot in front of the other and resist the horror of it all collapsing in on you.

It crushes some people. It crushes them and grinds them to powder.

Chapter Three

We fished most Sundays from one of any number of piers up and down the Pacific coast.

He wouldn't get interested in church for another three or four years and Clovis's was closed on Sundays, so typically he would get me around early and while she and the baby slept we would go to Winchell's donuts and he would get three of them in a little waxed-paper bag. One for him and one for her and one for me, and after he had perked a new pot of coffee he would wake her up and they would feed pieces of their donuts to Sean in his highchair and they would laugh and talk and then he would put his poles and tackle box in the trunk and we would set off for some pier.

There was an old man named Leroy who washed dishes at Clovis's. He would die within a year or two and we would spend Sunday afternoons in his room in the months before he passed, the adults playing cards and us kids being seen but not heard. But in the first-grade he was still working and most Sundays he would meet us with his rod and reel and a pail of bait in an ocean-side parking lot for the walk out onto a pier he knew was good.

Black people knew about fishing, my step-father said, and Leroy was our guide. He had come from Down South a long time ago, after a problem in his town, and he had learned how to fish these new waters. We fished for the same reason he did - to fill our bellies. To come back with more than we'd had when we started. Not for sport, but for food, to take some of the bounty of the sea and fry it in a coating of eggs and cracker crumbs. They would go out some nights and scoop up the grunion when they came to breed, but mostly it was all day Sunday in the California sun, the cry of gulls and the mixture of accents and the downwind scent of Lucky Strikes and White Owls.

Most often we went to the Santa Monica Pier. Because it was the closest, because it was the best, because it was the one she had seen in a movie Back East, with the carousel, and when she had to get out she wanted to go someplace alive and special, someplace that had been in the movies. And that was the Santa Monica Pier. We never went to the carousel, but we drove past it once or twice a week, there in the big hippodrome, on the way home mostly, detouring down Colorado Avenue and driving out the length of the pier to make the turnaround by the bait shop, smelling the new-caught fish and the sweetness of the sea. It was a wonder outside the window, and we were in the doubled-back line of cars taking it all in, his fleshy arm resting in the open window, his hand atop the chrome mirror, she pursing her lips with nervous energy, craning her neck to see something interesting we had passed, black cat-eye glasses accenting her face. Sean and I were in the backseat, in the era before seatbelts, he usually asleep and wrapped in a blanket, I on my knees looking out the side window or crawled up in the back window.

There is something about the backseat of your parents' car. At least there was in those days, before restraints and child-safety seats and government regulations about which way you can face and how much you must weigh and how old you must be before you can be free to sit in a car the way you wish. Before it is your parents who decide instead of the state. In those days, at the end of a drive or the end of a day, in the back seat of your parents' car, as you became drowsy, you simply laid out across the back seat and drifted into a sleep based on the premise that all was right in the world and you were safe in it. The steady vibration and the hum, the half-heard snippets of their conversation, the thumps and bumps and lurches of potholes and turns and creases in the pavement. If there is peace in life, it is there, as a little boy, sleeping in the backseat of your parents' car.

Of course, you can't drive away from your problems, with a move across the country or a pleasure ride down to Venice or Marina Del Rey. And the front seat may be different from the back, it may be a place of weightier issues, of suffocating responsibilities, of two people who love one another and the wind in their hair but who face together the terror of a pile of bills and the tyranny of income versus outgo. Two people whose gossamer dreams flap and fray in the gales of reality. Two people who work in a diner, with sleeping hungry boys in the backseat in need of shoes and coats.

It was on Santa Monica Pier that I caught the herring. It was a good-sized fish. I usually caught fish, but small fish, any one of the various anonymous species that cluster around the pilings and strip the fishermen's hooks. But one Sunday, in mid-afternoon, I caught a herring, on a little hand line he had baited for me. He had baited it and told me to drop it over and he and Leroy had rigged their respective poles and cut the smelts just right and cast them out in hopes of catching some mackerel or croakers, or maybe a halibut or a bonito, any one of the fish that would hopefully before we went home be gutted and filleted on the big common table and wrapped in the "Evening Outlook" to be our dinner in the coming week. The line was braided, in those days before monofilament, and was coarse and green and strong, and wrapped end over end on a rectangular spool. It had a sinker and a hook and a bobber and the smell of rotting kelp.

I unspooled enough line to reach the water, and stretching out between the pier railings, the rigging hanging from my hand, I flung it into space. It dropped with a paired splash in the water between the pilings, and as I fed it more line it slowly floated forward and back as the vagaries of the waves pushed it one way or another. Leroy chewed a cigar and talked about the big run of white sea bass they had once, about the time I was born, and how they pulled them in that year. Big fish, huge fish, hundreds of them. You couldn't help but catch them. Right on this pier here, Leroy said, they were catching those fish till the cows came home. Those were the days, Leroy said. He ate good then. Everybody ate good then.

It was my step-father on one side with his two poles, Leroy on the other side with his two poles, me in the middle with my hand line, and rows of other men stretching along the pier in either direction. Some where white, many were black, another many were Chinese, all were staring intently at the water, or out to sea, or at tangled reels, trying to sort out back-lash and confusion.

There is something primal about fishing, primal and predatory. Back home, on the TV on Monday nights, Andy and Opie whistled happily on their father-and-son outing to the lake. It was relaxed and casual, and it remains that in folk-lore, in the suppositions of people who don't do it. It's a happy, lazy time of camaraderie with friends and communing with nature. Except, in reality, it's not. In reality, it's a tense waiting, a nuanced stalking, an uncertain moment-to-moment anticipation of a jerk on your line. The rapid grab of a run or the slight pull of an easy take, the mystical bite, as something unseen bumps or mouths or grabs your bait below. Your thoughts may drift, the conversation may wander, but a part of your mind, the vigilant part, is focused on the feel of the line between your fingers and the dance of your bobber upon the water. You will feel the wind and you will feel the waves and your mind will think it feels something more, in the lapping of water and the stretching of line, and then there will be something different. A bite. A quick tug, a submerged bobber, and you pull back. Sometimes hard. To set the hook. To pull that bait back, as the fish works to swallow it, and bury the point and then the barb in its mouth. You can feel right away if it worked. If it's easy and straight, through clean water, it got away, you pulled it out of its mouth, and you've lost. But if it's heavy and fighting, if the line goes taut and the fish tries to run, then you've got it, and the struggle is on. It's you against the fish, and if you play it right, if your gear holds, if it doesn't work out of its mouth, odds are you lift it splashing and spent up over the top rail of the pier and you've got one. And it gets thumped and thrown in a box and that's all she wrote. You won, it lost, you're alive, it's not. This was before catch and release, this was when any such notion would have been laughed off the pier. If you didn't want it, the thinking would have gone, why did you catch it? The fish got dead, you got fed, that's why you stood out there in the sun.

That mackerel bite was like that.

I was looking down at the bobber, as it rocked on the water, the line wrapped twice around my palm and held between my index finger and thumb, when all of a sudden the bobber danced and the string jerked and I jerked back and shrieked in glee and surprise that I had a bite.

Kids do that when they fish, which is one of the reasons adults don't like to take them fishing. They yell and they don't know how to do things and it becomes babysitting and stops being fishing. There are lines to tangle and reels to break and hooks to misplace and generally fishing children do little more than move from one screw up to another. Which might have been why I was using a hand line and was patronizingly dismissed when I got the bite. A passive "Did you get it?" and a "Give it some line" and a "We'll check it in a minute" and I was left on my own and ignored as the bobber danced again and jerked and I jerked back and then nothing.

But maybe not nothing. In the uncertainty of hope and confusion, was it the steady pull of wind or was it the slight wobble of water or was it the resistant drag of a fish? It went on that way for a time. It would jerk, or so I thought, and I would jerk back. And my bobber would settle into to its rhythmic ride on the waves and after a time I would think I felt it again and I would jerk it a bit and sometimes I would just raise the line to watch the water run back down it and to see the splash of the bobber as I dropped it from a foot or two above the water.

It may have been a couple of hours later before he said it was pointless and we might as well go home. He and Leroy began to reel in and gather up our stuff and I began wrapping my line around its spool. I hadn't done much more than take the slack out of it before it became hard, and pulling the line up from the water became too difficult, and I said I needed help. I was hooked on the pilings, he said, or maybe hung up in some kelp, and he walked over to try to free the line. As he took it and leaned over the rail and lifted the line above his head, we first saw the mackerel rise toward the surface. It was essentially motionless, of fairly good size, and completely entangled in my line. As it had taken the bait and been hooked, its struggles and my jerking had wrapped the line around its body, each loop seemingly more restrictive than the last, until it was trapped, unable to move except for the alternate opening of its gill covers and mouth. He and Leroy laughed and slapped me on the back and called over some of the Chinese men they had been visiting with to see. He pulled it up and untangled it and Leroy cleaned it for me on the big common table and that night she fried it in a coating of eggs and cracker crumbs.

I saw that fish for years in my mind, tangled in my line as he pulled it to the surface. At first, it was a vision of glory, a conquest and victory, a childhood adventure that ended in joy. The day I caught our supper. But as I aged, I thought less of the glory, and more of the line, and of the fish enmeshed in the strangling tangles, caught up not by my strength, but by the accumulating restraint of suffocating bondage.

As I aged, I identified less with the boy, and more with the fish.

We are born to swim free, to make our way as we can, but responsibility and its perversion, worry, hook us and turn us and encircle us about, each struggle or run to be free bringing another loop and another restraint and another step closer to the servitude of circumstance.

Chapter Four

They came for the car early in the morning, while she was still in her housecoat.

She stood on the grass between the sidewalk and the street and sobbed, her face in her hands. I stood silently beside her, spelling the word "repossession" frantically over and over in my head. I could not understand it, I could not stop it, I only knew it hurt her and that it was bad. He had caught a ride to work that day, so she could be there to send me to school, and now she couldn't go to work, so she stayed home that day and when I got back from school she had chopped her hair with scissors and bleached it yellow with peroxide.

In later years, she would have gone away for a time, for a month or two, and we would have stayed with my aunt or my grandmother or the county would have sent some woman to watch us. That was after he died, after we went Back East, before the drinking started, when she was a widow with four kids and not yet 30 years old. In those years, and the ones that followed, after I had grown and gone, it would happen and the police would take her and she would always be grateful when it was the state troopers, as they would treat her with kindness, and not make her wear the handcuffs. For that reason, I appreciate the state troopers to this day.

But then, all she could do was bleach her hair and lay on the couch and cry.

She was a very thin woman, when I was in the first-grade, because she was young and because she didn't eat. Oh, she ate, of course, but not very much, and not every day. She had big cracks in her lips and when she asked the baby doctor about it, the one who gave Sean his shots, he said it was probably malnutrition. That was Doctor Levine. He was Jewish. She insisted on a Jewish doctor for her kids. Black people know how to fish, they believed, and Jewish people know how to doctor, and Back East the doctor in town had been Irish and everybody loved him but there weren't any Jewish people so they had to take what they could get. But California was different and when Sean was born and had to get his check-up she picked Doctor Levine because he was Doctor Levine. She paid him in rolled quarters and dimes and was completely satisfied that, no matter what she went without, she had gotten her children the best of medical care.

The car they took wasn't much, but it was ours. In the sense of possession and affection, it belonged to us, no matter what the paperwork said. A lien is a theory, a politely ignored fact, an asterisk to ownership that essentially means, "not really." A car loan or a mortgage allows the benefit of ownership, and the usefulness of ownership, without the certainty and security of ownership. It is a hopefully permanent tenancy, which may end up being more hopeful than permanent.

He and I washed it each Saturday morning. A hose and a bucket and some soap and a couple of rags. He got the high parts and I got the low parts and he teased me and told me stories and talked about a new Mustang he had seen and asked about school, while the radio played through the open window. "King of the Road" and "I've Got a Tiger by the Tail," "I Got You Babe" and "Yesterday." We smeared wax on and then buffed it off with a cloth, and when we were done she and Sean would climb in with us and we would drive north up the Pacific Coast

Highway to see the sea, or south to see John Wayne's yacht. The car was ours. It was our family's.

And early one morning while she was still in her housecoat two men came and took it away.

When he got home that night, a neighbor drove us to a small car lot lit by lights on a wire and he gave the salesman his gun and their wedding rings and a promise of so much a month. It was a loud car and we carried a case of oil in the trunk. She cried on the way home that night, and I heard her cry on their fold-out bed in the living room while I lay on the top bunk around the corner in the closet. Two years later they would hit a hard spell, after she had had Peter and spilled the scalding coffee on her legs tending the counter at the Rexall, and we would move every month or two, avoiding the repo men and the angry landlords. But that night, a promise of so much a month was easy to make, if not to keep, and the next morning, after I'd gone to school, she drove that loud car in to Clovis's and everyone talked about her new hair.

Chapter Five

Neither one of them had had a TV growing up. He had come up before it was available and she had come up before it was affordable, at least in her mother's house, and the small-screen black-and-white in the living room was a treat for them, a treat for us all, and in the evenings, in the payoff of the day, we sat, the four of us, on the couch, watching the world in a little box. This was back when horizontal hold meant something and how you twisted the rabbit ears and how much snow you could take. They played "Peter Pan" with Mary Martin that year and most days I saw "Romper Room" and "Captain Kangaroo," and "Diver Dan" and maybe "Felix the Cat."

But family time was TV time and in the evenings we invariably sat, him with his arm around her, her with her arm around me, and Sean in the crook of someone's arm, in front of the TV. It gave us something to share, it gave us something to talk about, it gave us something to remember. And it played out on a predictable schedule, this show on that night and that storyline picked up after this day's work.

Two men were stars in our home - Dick Lane and Cal Worthington.

Dick Lane came in two or three nights a week, from the Olympic Auditorium, with wrestling and boxing and roller derby. It was Bobo Brazil and The Sheik, Freddie Blassie and Mil Mascaras, and the four of us, yelling and cheering and flinching with the blows and antics, Dick Lane providing straight-faced commentary and the occasional "Whoa, Nellie!" One night wrestling and another night roller derby and the third night boxing. It was the Los Angeles T-Birds versus the Bay Area Bombers and around and around they would skate, decked by elbows and slung off of the track. Big Amazon women and athletic aspiring starlets, in search of their own streets paved with gold, interviewed by Dick Lane at the end of the show. Fights would invariably break out and one night with Dick Lane in between two hulking athletes there were punches thrown and the sound of furniture breaking and the screen went blank and then, almost quietly, Dick Lane saying, "I'm hit." A pause. "I'm hit low." And it went to commercial as we sat there, mouths open in shock, fearing the worst.

It was wrestling, boxing and roller derby, and sometimes bullfighting in Spanish from Mexico, all sports of battle and conquest. Little morality plays in black and white, of good guys versus bad guys and strong versus weak. We took it all at face value, accepted it all as real, shared it all as a family. And sometimes in the routine of the day she would grab me and give me a Coco Butt or with feigned fierceness throw me to the couch and put me in a Camel Clutch, tickling under my arms as she did. He would randomly put a bowl on his head and run, either through our home or past the counter in Clovis's, shouting "The jam is on!" and she would laugh her hearty way and squeal as he, pretending to skate after her with his elbows flying, would eventually catch her and kiss her and skate on.

This was 20 years after the Second World War. His boyhood had been spent in the Depression and her first years were lived with ration coupons, and theirs was an America of possibilities. Rather, theirs was an America bereft of impossibilities. America had destroyed one world and was building another. It had torn down tyranny and was spreading forth freedom.

The American Way was the right way and the pastimes were what they had always been, metaphors for life and its struggles, object lessons in which good was rewarded and tenacity prevailed. Winners never quit and quitters never win, and good guys come out on top. It was the spirit of America, it was the spirit of Los Angeles, it was the spirit of the westward wind that had brought so many of these people from Back East and Down South, to go 30 rounds with a fate that would undoubtedly bloody them and put them down for a two-count more than once, lay them on their backs and give them every chance to quit. But which promised them, if they would simply keep fighting - if they would never quit, never quit, never quit - they would come out on top. Life is as simple as that. Persist and prevail. If you persist, you will prevail. If you don't quit, you will win. Discouragement whispers that that is a lie, faith shouts that it is a truth. Hope clings through dark nights to the latter, while it quakes in fear of the former. Choice and time, in the striped shirt of reality, stand ready to lift one hand or the other in victory.

She often had difficulty sleeping, and after Sean was

in his crate and the couch was folded out and he was snoring asleep, she would lie there with the television playing low, hour after hour, and too lonely to be alone she would often call out to see if I was awake. When I was, I would come and snuggle in beside her and we would watch "Star Trek," or "Perry Mason" repeats or old movies, until we dozed off, half waking more than once to see the Indian head on the test pattern. Through the night, in the breaks, Cal Worthington was our friend and entertainer. A tall thin man in a cowboy hat and a funny tie, he talked loud and smiled wide and invariably referenced, "My dog, Spot," which would be some exotic animal lounging at his feet or climbing on his back. He was selling cars and we were buying laughs and familiarity, and while the programs we watched sometimes faded from memory with the new day, his pitch and that particular Spot would be remembered and remarked upon, the topic of conversation or quip.

Television is invariably an escape. It brings nothing to you, it takes you to some thing or some place. To a feeling or a memory, an appetite or a lust, and you can master it or it will master you. It can enliven humankind, or enslave humankind.

It is less a picture and more a mirror, and what you get out of it invariably is a reflection of who you are. In those days, in that room, with those people, television was a friend and a bond, something we treasured and something we shared, something we laughed with or wept to. California is not a freeway, it is rows of glowing dots on the back of a curving sheet of glass.

Chapter Six

I can't remember if the paste was wintergreen or spearmint.

It was something minty and it came in a white plastic tub with several wooden tongue depressors sticking out of the top. It smelled good and it tasted good and on the days we would have art a tub would sit at each cluster of desks.
John Muir, the school that we all love the best. Down by the blue Pacific, we think it's real terrific. John Muir, the school that we all love the best.

That's what we sang. Each morning. We recited the Pledge of Allegiance and we sang the school song and at the corner of Ocean Park and Lincoln Boulevard we learned. It was not a long walk from home, but neither was it an easy walk from home. From the house you simply followed Ocean Park across the intersection at Beverly, up over the near crest of a hill and then down that hill between the fences and walls and the passing traffic, across 7th Street and on ultimately at the bottom of the hill to the school.

It seemed cold and wet that late autumn, especially for what I thought California would be. There were palm trees and sea gulls, but there were also clouds and rain, and in the morning I set off in a small sweater that bunched my shirtsleeves uncomfortably. I was really not quite capable of either reliably zipping the sweater or tying my shoes. Class was mostly simple math and the wonders of reading, with science and music and the "Weekly Reader." We broke into groups based on ability and I was always in the first group.

Our teacher was gracious and she always wore a dress, and was never cross or scolding. I've long since forgotten her name, but not her form or demeanor. She was the typical teacher of her day, prim and professional, reserved and right, teaching phonics and old math and love of goodness and country. Answers were right or wrong, facts were to be learned, tests were to be passed, good behavior was demanded. The approach of her generation of teachers has long been denounced, but never improved, and rarely matched. They taught the Baby Boom, and they taught me.

Through November and December we rehearsed for the Christmas Concert. Some classes sang carols and some classes rang bells and our class recited "Twas the Night Before Christmas." Some sang in Spanish and some sang in English and some sang in Latin and we stood, row on row on the bleachers, in the cherub voices of the small, reciting the words of Clement C. Moore. Naturally, we did poorly at first, butchering line upon line, but each afternoon, just before we went home, we stood in the courtyard on the bleachers, reciting what we knew and learning what we didn't, adding a line here and a line there until the stanzas came naturally in rolling unison.

It was just before the concert that we decorated the room and the tree.

A week or two before Christmas, it stood in the corner of the room, a surprising and delightful presence at the start of a day. Some sort of evergreen, trucked in from the mountains, nailed at its base to a cross member of white wood. We gathered around it in awe and excitement, till we were sent to our seats with the explanation that if our morning went well our afternoon would be dedicated to decoration.

Which brought us back happily from lunch, the paste pots on our desks and stacks of scissors and construction paper waiting for our use. The teacher stood before us and held up the paper and the scissors and showed us how to cut long strips, of red and green. When that was done, and there were hundreds of such strips, she held up a green one and rolled it round, so that one end touched the other, and affixed the two with a smear of paste from one of the wooden tongue depressors. Then she threaded a red strip through the green circle and rolled it likewise into a link, which she pasted, and told us to do the same, alternating colors, to make lengthening chains, Christmas garlands, of green and red.

When sufficient had been produced, most with the irregularities unavoidable from the elementary hand, smudged with wayward paste and smelling distinctly of mint, she stood eye to eye with the top of the tree and wrapped the red and green around and around. Excess adorned the frame of the door and the sills of the windows and the front of her desk. Then we were put to work making snowflakes from white squares of paper folded and refolded and cut helter skelter and taped around the blackboard or hung by loops of yarn from the boughs of the tree.

It was beautiful. It was electrifying.

It was Christmas as Christmas can only be in the first-grade. We sang "Jingle Bells" every day, and "Silent Night," and we wrote letters to Santa on penmanship paper with big, round pencils. Letters that had to be spelled right and formed properly and expressive of sufficient respect and gratitude. At snack time there would be hot cocoa or cookies, distributed around the tree, a moment's pause to admire the store-bought star at the top, and the soft scent of evergreen. And each afternoon, just before we put our coats on and lined up and walked out the door to go home, the teacher sat with us on the floor beside the Christmas tree and read us a story of the season. It was two weeks' work for a teacher, and a lifetime's memory for a child.

Chapter Seven

Rudolph the Red-Nosed Reindeer" was new then, and wondrous, and we watched it with the awe of discovery. At least I did. It was a masterwork of literature, as far as I was concerned, and every moment, word and note was delicious to me. It was an enzyme of anticipation, and left me bubbling and overflowing with eagerness for the approaching holiday.

There is a zeal in childhood, a complete, sprinting abandon, an open-armed embrace of happiness around the corner. It can be a birthday or the Tooth Fairy or the Easter Bunny, but most intensely it is Christmas. Christmas and Santa Claus and presents and food. Songs and decorations and the earnest belief that life is good.

The season had started the night before Thanksgiving with the Santa Claus Lane Parade. I watched it on television, seeing George Putnam and the Hollywood lights, and waited for Santa at the end. The next day would be the Macy's Thanksgiving Day Parade with Santa once again, and the season would be bookended by the Rose Parade, and we would drive down to Pasadena after to see the floats and their incredible flowers. But it was Rudolph, that year, that gave me the Christmas spirit, that lit me up with the season's joy.

It was after Rudolph, as she stood next to my bunk to tuck me in, that I told her I couldn't wait for Christmas.

It was after Rudolph, as she stood next to my bunk to tuck me in, that she told me there wasn't going to be a Christmas.

It didn't register. I was confused. I couldn't understand what she was saying.

No Christmas?

We can't afford Christmas this year, she said, we would have to wait till next year.

It wasn't any clearer for me. Christmas wasn't something that was afforded, Christmas was something that happened, like sun and rain and the rising tide.

I explained this to her, that she didn't have to worry, that Santa Claus would bring Christmas.

She was 24, she was mentally ill, she had no money,

she had no prospects, and her first-grader was assuring her that she had nothing to worry about. Santa Claus would take care of everything.

I heard her crying in the living room. He turned up Dick Lane with boxing from the Olympic so I wouldn't hear. She was crying because she didn't live in the world of "Miracle on 34th Street." She didn't live in the world of glass slippers and happy endings. She lived on a busy street in a dumpy house divided into three impossible apartments in a city famous for chewing people up and spitting them out. She was on the horrifying side of the divide between dreams and delusions. She was in the shadow of the realization that she had failed there and she had failed here and all she had run to was another set of disappointments on another side of the country.

She had just told her child that there would be no Christmas. Not because she wanted to, not because she could truly bear to, but because she had to, because it had been growing like a gathering storm, a darkening sky of dread, forced by math and the tyranny of income and out go. There was a looming intersection of hope and reality, like an uncontrolled crossing of two country roads, and with the collision coming faster and faster, she could ignore it no longer, she had to say what she had to say. And fearing she would break a little boy's heart, she broke her own.

He held her that night and smoothed her hair and listened to her sob. The weight of failure was heaviest on his shoulders. He was the man. He was the provider. He had asked for her hand and all that went with it. Her son called him Daddy and his own son lit up when he walked in the room. Their world was of his creation, or at least of his responsibility and as bad as she felt for her son, he felt for her, and Christmas wasn't very joyous after all.

I heard her cry and I heard Dick Lane and I heard his voice over the crowd at the Olympic. I knew what was happening around the corner of the room, but I didn't know why.

I just lay there reciting in my head, from beginning to end, over and over, "Twas the Night Before Christmas," certain of the storyline, certain of the point, certain of the promise. We nestle all snug in our beds, and St. Nick brings Christmas. The presents, the joy, the party, I had learned it in school. We sang songs, we made decorations, Christmas was coming. It had to.

Or maybe it didn't.

There is a dawning maturity in the first-grade mind, a pie-in-the-sky belief that everything works out, but the first honest observation that, in fact, it doesn't always. A first-grader is a child, but a child who is just half realizing that he will someday be an adult. A child who is just now having the hope beat out of him by the disappointment of life.

I wondered if she could be right. I wondered if Christmas could, indeed, pass us by. I wondered if Santa could simply fly over.

I thought of Kathryn Kuhlman, the preacher woman in the flowing robes on television. She waved her arms and raised her voice and said, "I believe in miracles!" Sunday mornings, while we ate our donuts, in the background as we talked, she shouted mostly ignored from the little set in the living room, "I believe in miracles!"

I didn't know what a miracle was, not by observation or faith. I knew who God was, and I prayed to him every night. Now I lay me down to sleep. I pray the Lord my soul to keep.

If I should die before I wake, I pray the Lord my soul to take. While staying with one aunt, I had gone to mass. While staying with another, I had gone to the Methodist Sunday school. While staying with my grandmother, we went to the Baptist church. I had a rough idea, but not a clear understanding. I knew there was a real meaning of Christmas and I knew that Santa Claus wasn't it, but I knew that Santa Claus was good and that God supported the good.

And I wondered if I could have a miracle. I wondered if God could send Santa Claus to my house.

Chapter Eight

She was in the movie for two days.

It was one of those friend-of-a-friend things. One of the regulars at Clovis's was talking about it and she heard and it was better than tip money and sounded like a great adventure so, after a phone call and with permission from Clovis, she caught the early morning bus they provided for the extras and went up to Lake Sherwood.

They put her in old clothes and made her take off her glasses and her watch and with dozens of others she was a villager in "What Did You Do In The War, Daddy?" For all the years since, in the crowd scenes, I have searched for her, and never found her, but both of the days she went up for the filming she came home with stories that fascinated us all. The two families from Down South and Chocolata's parents, and some people we knew from over by Los Amigos Park, crowded into our dining room both nights to hear about the cameras and the director and the waiting around. She waved like they showed them how to and spoke of seeing this actor and that, and marveled at how different movies were on the other side of the screen. We listened in wonder and interest, and I was so proud to be her son. When the others had left, she brought out the box lunch she had been given on the set and divided it between Sean and me, for our supper. The four of us sat at the table, on top of the world. She was in a movie.

That Saturday I stood with her at the payphone on the street. Calls were cheaper on the weekends then, and you paid three minutes at a time, and with the help of an operator and after the steady click of dropping dimes and connecting switches, there would be a ring and an answer and the operator announcing that she had a long-distance call for so and so. In this case, so and so was my grandmother, in her house out on the Willow Bend Road.

In 1972, Bennett's Creek, less than 100 yards away, would come out of its banks and wash the house and its history away. It had been built about 1820 and she had bought it after my grandfather had taken off and she was left with seven kids and no prospects. For a time they lived in a chicken coop in

Bishopville and then the bank gave her a note and she took all seven of them down across the Silver Bridge south of Canisteo and made a go of it. It was her and those kids and two mules named Jack and Jenny. For years, they lived on what they grew and a steady diet of cornmeal mush. They came through, but it made her a hard woman, or at least most of her children thought she was a hard woman, and I heard fear and apprehension in the voice at the payphone. There was talk about the movie and about the rent and about problems with Christmas. Then there was listening, and the dropping of more coins, and disappointment. The magic connection of wire and words, a brief glimpse home, old realities unchanged, no help for the holidays.

She hung up and we turned for home.

You must listen to each pleading voice. Some, in selfish entitlement, believe life is theirs for the asking, that they deserve to be carried about by the efforts and earnings of others. But others only ask when they need, and they wouldn't ask if they didn't need, and the rebuffed request is a blow indeed. So you must listen, and discern. Because none are faulted for refusing the greedy, but none are justified in declining the needy. The great challenge is in knowing which is which. Compassion is not foolishness, and neither is foolishness compassion. So you must listen, not just to the words of people, but to the whispering of God, to find the place where you alone may assist, where your particular hand and heart are needed. We are to bear one another's burdens, not to support the idle, but to save the destitute. Sometimes we will get it right, and sometimes we won't.

We walked home from the payphone past houses decorated with lights and trees. Plastic Santas stood in lawns next to sleighs and candy canes. Our rooms were unchanged, save for a Christmas card from Aunt Lonnie, standing on a doily as a centerpiece on the dining-room table.

In the cupboard, he had hidden a bag of popcorn, some confectioner's sugar, a bottle of Karo syrup and two tiny bottles of red and green food coloring. That was for the popcorn balls. He also had four oranges and some walnuts and filberts and a few pieces of hard candy. That was for the stockings. In those days, the stockings were socks, regular socks from your drawer, and they hung by nails somewhere, put up before bed on Christmas Eve, filled by Santa as you slept. He always put an orange in the toe, and it hung pendulously, and the rest was filled up with nuts and hard candy.

He figured if Santa had something for the stockings, and there were popcorn balls to wake up to on Christmas morning, that all would not be lost, and a young heart would not be broken, and a young family would not be left in gloom on the most joyous of days.

He was a good man, and I called him Daddy. Not because I wanted to at first, but because Sean needed to call him that, and hear him called that, and so I did. And each night from atop the bunk I would yell around the corner, “Good night, Daddy,” and he would yell, “Good night” back to me. It’s not that I grew up without a father, it’s that I grew up with too many fathers. A succession of them. But this one was good. He gave me the belt, but he also gave me his love, and he gave her the closest thing she ever had to happiness, and I hope to see him again on the other side. I hope then to yell out again, “Good night, Daddy,” and hear him call in return.

He used to comb my hair before bed, greased down in the fashion of his day, and say that I needed to look good when I met the girl of my dreams.

Decades later, I still run my tongue over the juncture of my top two front teeth. Just before he died, I had dawdled over a sinkful of dishes, playing instead of washing, and seeing this as he walked by, he cuffed me in the back of the head. I flew forward and, being 10 and just higher than the sink board, I struck my mouth on the porcelain, chipping the tooth. It was minor at the time and has worn smooth since, but I appreciate the lesson it taught. I remind myself of that lesson with the touch of my tongue, and I believe I have been better for it. You accomplish when you work, and you don't when you don't. And if he gave me nothing else, in the hardscrabble reality of life, that is not a bad legacy to have.

Chapter Nine

The last day of class before Christmas was a Thursday, the twenty-third. It was rainy and gray but I ran happily down the hill to school. The Christmas concert had been Tuesday night and our poem had gone off without a hitch and the place was alive with the spirit of the season. We had a special lunch on Thursday and our class party filled the afternoon. There were games and songs and cookies from a variety of mothers. A man came in dressed like Santa Claus and passed out pencils and tablets and candy canes. We finished construction-paper cards for our parents and went Christmas caroling to the kindergartners and the principal and the librarian.

Then it was time to go.

The afternoon was spent and the bell was about to ring and the classroom settled into its daily routine of departure. We got our sweaters and coats and gathered our papers and stood respectfully in a line extending from the door back along the wall beside our desks. When we were in order, and all was prepared, the teacher took her place by the door and turned off the light, and we stood quietly waiting to be dismissed.

We did that that day. We did that every day. But that day I did something different. I stepped out of line and walked up to the teacher.

I didn't do such things. I was a good student, and I had plenty of friends, but I was essentially shy, and I did not misbehave. It would not have occurred to me to be different or disobedient, to draw negative attention to myself or to get in trouble of any kind. I had wet my pants in kindergarten, and gotten beaten for it, and had had great difficulty learning to tie my shoes, and I felt self-conscious about myself and my failings. Years later, after he had died and we had gone Back East, as I walked down the streets of my hometown, I was so bashful that if I saw someone coming down the sidewalk toward me, I would cross the street so as not to have to greet them in my awkwardness. But I got out of line and walked to the door and met the teacher's eyes as I approached her.

"What is going to happen to the Christmas tree?" I said.

It was still in the corner, with the store-bought star at the top, encircled by our red-and-green construction-paper chains and splashed with white-paper snowflakes.

"The custodian will throw it away over the break," she said.

"May I have it?"

She looked at me curiously.

"Why do you want it?"

"Because we're not having Christmas this year. Santa's not coming to our house."

"What makes you say that?"

"My mother told me. She said we can't afford to have Christmas this year."

The teacher looked at me.

"And you want to take the tree home so you can have Christmas?"

"Yes."

"How will you get it home?"

"I will drag it home. I can do it easy."

She paused, the bell rang, she opened the door and in

a flurry of Merry Christmases my classmates filed out.

"OK," she said. "You can have it."

It was difficult for her and the needles were dry and prickly, but she reached in, grabbed the tree by the trunk at about chest level, lifted it up and awkwardly carried it out the door and down the hall to the front entrance of the school.

"There you go," she said. "Merry Christmas."

With that she went back into the school and I stood there, next to the tree, looking up at it, imagining how proud my mother would be of me. It was windy and starting to rain and the decorations fluttered in the breeze.

I pushed it over, grabbed hold of the cross-member X nailed onto the base of the trunk, and pulled it with difficulty down the five steps in front of the school and out the few feet to the sidewalk.

It was heavier than I had imagined it would be, and large and ungainly, and I could pull it a stride or two or three before I would need to stop and get a better grip and try it again.

Ocean Park Boulevard from John Muir School toward

our house went uphill most of the way, at a fairly steep grade, a fact that worked powerfully against me, and was compounded by the gusting wind which pushed the tree this way and that, and tore its decorations. My progress was very slow, a foot or two at a time, the tree every bit as wide as I was tall, my thin first-grade frame lacking the strength to truly move it. After great effort, and a fair amount of time, I had moved the relatively short distance to the intersection with 7th Street.

This posed a great problem for me, as the street was wide and had regular traffic, and were I to try to drag the tree across it, I would need to stop and rest, probably three or four times, in the middle of the road. I was stuck. And I stood there, unsure what to do. The light rain had dampened my sweater and my hair, I was starting to feel a chill. I was stuck.

A car going west on Ocean Park slowed to turn right onto 7th, made the turn and pulled to the curb. The woman driving opened her door and stood up and in a raised voice asked if I needed some help. I said that I needed to get the tree across the street but I couldn't. So she got out, came over, grabbed the cross member with one hand and taking my hand with the other, pulled the tree across 7th to the far corner. She asked if that was better and I said it was and I thanked her and she wished me a merry Christmas and she went back to her car.

Ocean Park continues up a steep grade until it crests at Highland Avenue. It took me more than an hour to get there. Back along my path there were random needles and shredded decorations. The red-and-green chain was tatters, the snowflakes were sodden, I was soaked to the skin. My hands were splintered and sore.

I had never known anything so difficult, I have not since done anything so physically demanding. It was a journey of inches and impossibilities. Of discouragement and tears. Of wanting to quit and not knowing how to go forward, driven on by the simple fact that I had Christmas in my hands - I had happiness in my hands - that this had to be done, and that it had to be done by me. I could have Christmas, but I could not have it for free. A couple of times I stopped to cry, I repeatedly readjusted my grip, I pulled most times and the tree did not move.

But I did not quit.

Pulling the tree up that hill may not be the defining point of this story, but it was a defining event in my life.

After the crest at Highland, Ocean Park levels and by the time I got to Beverly there was a slight descent. Beverly seemed less heavily trafficked than 7th, and after waiting a few minutes on the curb, I pulled the tree a lurching foot or two into the street, and continued in that fashion to the far curb, two cars coming during that time and slowing to drive around me.

A few more sidewalk squares and I was home, outside the front stoop. I was exhausted, I was shivering, I was exhilarated. Standing there in the drizzling rain, I was happiest boy. I had a Christmas tree, and I had it home. I had accomplished something, I had helped my family, my mother would be so proud of me.

They wouldn't be home for another couple of hours, and I was afraid to leave the tree unattended, for fear it would be stolen, so I stood there beside it, smiling, vainly thinking that the passing motorists thought I must be quite some boy indeed. I was horribly cold, but completely content, and glad to continue paying the price for this tree.

I was standing there in the dark when the loud car slowed for the turn onto Beverly. I could see their faces in surprise and puzzlement. She took Sean in the back door and he walked around the corner on the sidewalk, in his houndstooth cook's pants, and asked, "What have you here?" She opened the front door from the inside and he picked up the tree and carried it in.

I told the story as she stripped off my wet clothes and started to draw a bath. He moved the television and its stand from their place and set up the tree in the corner of the living room, where its side would be visible from my bunk. He picked off the unsalvageable construction-paper decorations and dried the store-bought star with a towel. After dinner, she said it was too bad we didn't have any popcorn to string to decorate the tree. He said that maybe we did, and retrieving the hidden bag there was soon the smell of hot oil and the thunderous popping of the corn, and he had gone next door to borrow from the neighbors the leftovers of a bag of cranberries.

Around the coffee table in front of the couch, we bent, each a needle and thread in hand, to string garlands of popcorn and cranberries, red and white, several kernels and a berry, several kernels and a berry, several kernels and a berry. Sean tottered repeatedly to the heaping bowl of popcorn, bringing handfuls to his mouth and yammering happily, we laughed at him and they told stories and we sang carols and I recited "Twas the Night Before Christmas." As each strand got to a good length, we would wrap it around the tree, from the top to the bottom, the three of us, passing it around and around, reaching where we could.

As I tired and the job was complete, we sat back on the couch, his arm around her, her arm around me, Sean in the crook of someone's arm, looking at our beautiful tree, wrapped in white and red, its store-bought star at the top.

I fell asleep there and he carried me finally to my bunk while she gently changed a sleeping Sean and laid him down in the crate beneath me.

Chapter Ten

I half awoke the next morning, long before the sun, to the sound of popping corn in the kitchen. It made no sense, and I repositioned myself and fell back asleep.

He was alone at the stove, in his T-shirt and boxers, hurrying to make the popcorn balls while the rest of us slept. He would form them, and wrap them, and hide them away, his secret Christmas, and slide back into their fold-out bed before she awoke.

It was a quiet day. Clovis's was closed, and after a walk down to Jocelyn Park we watched a movie on television and she made deviled eggs for the picnic the next day at Palisades Park with the people from Down South. People from Down South and Back East loved to picnic on Christmas. It was so California. It was something to write back home about, to take pictures of.

Imagine, a place where it is warm enough to picnic on Christmas. Instead of shoveling snow or staying in to be warm, California people go outside to picnic under palm trees next to the sea.

The plan was to go out with the neighbors on Christmas afternoon and we were supposed to bring the deviled eggs and while she was making those in the middle of the afternoon on Christmas Eve, there was a knock at the back door.

I stood up off the couch and looked through the dining room to see who it was.

He was at the door, opening it, and there were two men, in suits and ties, and they each held a large box.

They said they were from my teacher's church.

A few words were exchanged and he thanked them and took a box in each arm and closed the door and turned back toward the dining room, where he set the boxes on the table. She came from the kitchen and I came from the living room and we converged in wonder and awe.

One box was packed tight with presents, wrapped in Christmas paper with ribbons and bows. Large presents and small presents, labeled Mom or Dad, Big Brother or Little Brother. The other box was food. A large fresh turkey, and Brussels sprouts, sweet potatoes and squash. A can of black olives, a can of cranberry sauce, a jar of gravy and a bag of potatoes. A mincemeat pie and some flour for rolls. The makings of a feast with plenty left over.

There was also, in with the food, a small box of Christmas-tree decorations and a string of lights. While she put the perishables in the refrigerator, he and I untangled the lights and then strung them around as she helped Sean hang the glass ornaments.

When it was done and the afternoon was sliding into the early dusk of the season, we turned off the lights and sat in the dark, happy in the glow of the tree. It was a joy beyond imagining. Later, as bedtime came and went and I was excitedly awake, we hung our stockings and she tucked me into my bunk and told me to go to sleep so Santa could come. I told her I would but knew that I wouldn't and rolled over on my side so I could lie there and watch the half of the tree visible to me. Its colored lights and dangling ornaments and beautiful garlands were presided over by the store-bought star on the top. As my eyes grew heavy and flickered, each time I roused I was looking at the tree. When morning came, the very early morning best known by children on Christmas day, something was different. There were, placed around the base of the tree, presents. Large presents and small presents wrapped in Christmas paper with ribbons and bows, labeled Mom or Dad, Big Brother or Little Brother.

And on the table was a big bowl of popcorn balls, some red and some green. The stockings hung heavy with nuts, an orange in the toe.

I flew down from my bunk as if I was electricity. I picked Sean out of his crate and as he stretched and blinked I ran around the corner and up onto their fold-out bed, shouting as I did.

Santa came, I said, we are going to have Christmas. Santa came.

Indeed he had.

And God had helped him.

And there never was a better Christmas day.

I can't remember what was in the presents, but I'll never forget how they made me feel. It wasn't about things, it was about joy, the innocent, hopeful joy of a child. A joy that is available throughout life, but which can be painfully rare. I still love popcorn balls, and I'm jarred when there isn't an orange in the toe of the stocking. When I think of childhood Christmases, I think of the first-grade, and the Christmas that almost wasn't.

I can still see the lights of that tree from the bunk where I laid. I can still remember how Sean ripped the paper and stared happily transfixed at the tree. I can still remember how completely happy she was that day, and how joyously he smiled.

Peter was conceived that week, Christmas was saved that year, my life was bettered that day.

Of course, nothing fundamentally changed. The car still ran loud, they still worked at Clovis's, there still wasn't enough to go around. Life then, and in the years that followed, would continue to have its double portion of woe and discouragement. Night school, taken in turn while the other watched us, would give them each better jobs, and get us an apartment completely our own, and let them buy a genuinely new vehicle. But death and addiction and disease and death again would haunt the narrative, and just when things looked good, they would turn bad again. In this life, for either of them, there was very little peace.

And yet, that is the nature of life. And the realization of that is not a cause for despair. Rather, it is greater cause for the appreciation of the good. The forecast of tomorrow's rain should not curtail the enjoyment of today's sun. Rather, it should enhance it. The negative of life should not be allowed to swallow the positive. In times of struggle and trial, there are occasions for gratitude and joy. They should not be suffocated by struggle and trial, they should be highlighted by them. We can't appreciate the good without knowing the bad, and properly seen, the contrast magnifies and sweetens the good. The fact that life's pearls are rare, does not mean that they should not be collected and strung together and worn as the adornment of our existence.

Jobs will be lost, marriages will end, sicknesses will come and money will be scarce. Tears will be shed and hearts will be broken. And how foolish are we if we see these things as defining or damning. We are not our pay stubs or how the stock market performed yesterday. The economy can tank, the roof can leak, and still life can be great. There will be moments of happiness and hope, and they will make everything else worthwhile, and to find them all we have to do is continue.

Just go forward. Just don't quit.

Just believe.

And keep dragging that tree.

About the Author

Bob Lonsberry is a radio talk-show host who has worked as a newspaper columnist and reporter.

A former Mormon missionary and decorated veteran of the U.S. Army, he is a native of Canisteo, New York. He lives in Mount Morris, New York, the birthplace of Francis Bellamy and John Wesley Powell. He is married and is the father of eight children.

This is his seventh book.